The Princess and the Pea

Retold by Margo Lundell
Illustrated by Nan Brooks

A GOLDEN BOOK • NEW YORK
Golden Books Publishing Company, Inc., Racine, Wisconsin 53404

*O*nce there was a prince who wanted to marry a princess. However, she had to be a *real* princess, and nothing less would do.

Princesses of all kinds traveled from neighboring kingdoms to meet the prince. For one reason or another, the prince did not believe that the young women were truly princesses, and he sent them all away.

The queen, who was the prince's mother, offered to help. "Let me talk to the princesses," she said. "I will find out if they are real."

The stubborn prince shook his royal head. "No, Mother," he said. "I must find out by myself."

Finally no more princesses came to the palace, so the prince decided to go on a journey.

"If I must, I will search the world over for a princess," said the prince.

"We will miss you," said his father sadly.

The queen just waved good-bye, shaking her head over the whole business.

The prince traveled to France. There he was introduced to *la princesse* Mirabelle, who lived in a huge château.

"*Enchantée* to meet you," said the lovely princess as they sat to have tea.

During tea Princess Mirabelle ate nine chocolate truffles. The prince was shocked. He was sure that a real princess would never eat nine chocolate truffles in a row, and so he bade Mirabelle *adieu*.

The prince traveled and traveled until he came to Arabia. There he met a great pasha's daughter, Princess Morgiana.

The prince went riding with Morgiana, and she rode very well. But the princess did not ride sidesaddle, which was the ladylike custom.

"Morgiana sits on a horse like a man," the prince said to himself. "Surely she is not a real princess. I must take my leave."

Finally the prince arrived in India. There he met the daughter of a great raja.

As they spoke together, Princess Indira reached for grapes from a fruit bowl.

The prince sighed. "The princess did not ask her servant to peel the grapes before she ate them," he said to himself. "Surely she is not a real princess. I will have to say farewell."

The prince returned home. Looking most unhappy,
he told the king and queen that he could not find a real
princess anywhere in the world.

"I'm so sorry, my boy," said the king, trying to
comfort his son.

The queen just shook her head and wondered if the
day would ever come when her son would ask for her help.

One night soon afterward, there was a terrible storm. Lightning flashed through the castle, and rain poured down on the rooftops.

As the king was crossing the great hallway, he heard a knock on the door. "Who's there?" he called, going to open the door himself.

There stood a beautiful young woman, soaked from head to dainty toe.

"Won't you come in?" said the king.

"You are most kind," the dripping girl answered. "I have lost my way in this storm. My name is Princess Candice Alicia Royale."

The king hurried the princess inside and then sent for the prince to come and meet her.

The prince thought Princess Candice was charming. "But how can I be sure she is a real princess?" he whispered to his father.

"Perhaps you should ask your mother," the king whispered back. The prince agreed and went at last to ask his mother for help.

The queen liked the girl immediately.

"You poor tired thing," she said to the princess. "Won't you stay for the night?"

When Candice Alicia agreed, the queen went to prepare a bed for her.

First the queen ordered the servants to strip the princess's bed.

"Now we shall find out if Candice Alicia is a real princess," said the queen, and she carefully placed a single pea in the center of the bed frame.

After that the queen ordered the servants to pile ten thick mattresses on top of the bed and ten heavy quilts on top of the mattresses. Then a servant went and brought the princess.

"Your bed is ready, my dear,"
said the queen. "I do hope you
will be comfortable."

That night the princess was *not* comfortable. Hour after hour the exhausted creature tossed and turned. "Oh me, oh my," the princess moaned.

To help herself sleep,
the princess tried counting castles.

She tried counting handsome princes, too,
but nothing helped Candice Alicia to fall asleep.

The next morning the queen invited the princess
to breakfast. "My dear, did you sleep well?" she asked,
holding her breath for the answer.

"I scarcely slept at all," Candice-Alicia replied wearily. "I
lay on something so hard that I am black and blue all over."

The queen looked surprised, but she could not have
been more delighted.

The queen quickly told the prince what had happened. "Candice Alicia is a gem," she said at last. "Anyone delicate enough to feel a pea through ten quilts and ten mattresses is a *real* princess."

The prince was relieved. He smiled warmly at Candice Alicia. Before the day was over, he and the princess were in love.

Before a month had passed, the young couple was married. The royal wedding was a dazzling affair. The king's subjects loved their new princess. They also loved the story of the princess and the pea and told the story to their children for many years to come.

As for the pea itself, it was put on
display in the royal museum. You may see
it there still, if someone hasn't taken it.
And that, of course, is a true story.